FANCY PANTS

ALSO BY DAWN QUIGLEY

Jo Jo Makoons:
The Used-to-Be Best Friend

LEY

FANCY PANTS

ILLUSTRATED BY
TARA AUDIBERT

Heartdrum
An Imprint of HarperCollinsPublishers

Heartdrum is an imprint of HarperCollins Publishers.

Jo Jo Makoons: Fancy Pants
Text copyright © 2022 by Dawn Quigley
Illustrations copyright © 2022 by Tara Audibert
All rights reserved. Printed in the United States of America.
No part of this book may be used or reproduced in any manner whatsoever
without written permission except in the case of brief quotations embodied
in critical articles and reviews. For information address HarperCollins
Children's Books, a division of HarperCollins Publishers, 195 Broadway,
New York, NY 10007.
www.harpercollinschildrens.com

Library of Congress Control Number: 2021950885
ISBN 978-0-06-301540-1 (trade bdg.)
ISBN 978-0-06-301541-8 (pbk.)

Typography by Andrea Vandergrift
22 23 24 25 26   PC/LSCC   10 9 8 7 6 5 4 3 2 1

First Edition

To the real Auntie Anne and Uncle Jeffery:
Love you to Wisconsin and back.
—DQ

To all Indigenous little girls who never got
to see themselves in storybooks.
—TA

ABOUT THIS STORY

Jo Jo lives on a fictional Native American Ojibwe reservation, the Pembina Ojibwe Reservation. A reservation is land under the care of a Native Nation that calls it home. The land now called the United States is home to more than three hundred reservations and over five hundred Tribal Nations. There are many reservations in the United States, but Jo Jo's is not an actual one. Every reservation has unique and special elements, and Jo Jo's reservation incorporates many of those found in Ojibwe (and many other Native American) communities.

KOKUM

MIMI

MAMA

CHUCK

JO JO

FERN

PENNY

BRIE

FERRIS

TEACHER

AUNTIE ANNE

JEFFERY

CONTENTS

Mail Call

"Mimi, stay here. You're too little to cross the street alone. Somebody has to hold your hand. And I need to have empty hands right now," I said.

It was four o'clock in the afternoon. That meant it was time for me to go get the mail. Getting the mail is my job after I come home from school. Teacher told us there is a law that says kids cannot work until they are teenagers. Mama must not know this. I work a lot, only she calls it "chores" instead of work.

It is very important to be safe when you cross the street. You always need to look both ways.

I live on Eighth Street. This means I need to turn and look side to side eight times before I step into the street.

Left. Right. Left. Right. Left. Right. Left . . . Right. It is good to hold your arms straight out to balance when you are looking both ways. If you don't you get can spinny head.

I am very glad I don't live on 108th Street like my best school friend, Fern. That would hurt my neck. And is a very lot of counting.

"Mama!" I yelled when I got back in the house. "*He* wrote to you again."

"Jo Jo, who wrote to me?" Mama asked.

Mama looked at the letters. Bill sends a lot of letters to Mama. Then each month she looks at them all and gives a big puffy-outie breath. *Pfffff.* Mama's eyebrows get smushed when she reads his letters. She must not like him.

But she writes back all the time. She even sends him money!

That Bill guy. He writes a lot of letters.

"Mama, are there any letters for me?"

"No. But Jo Jo, do you ever write letters to anyone?" Mama answered.

"Well, last year I wrote one to Mimi when I was sick in bed, but she never wrote back."

My name is Jo Jo. You can call me Jo Jo. I am seven years old and in the first grade. Which is funny because I never went to zero grade, only kindergarten. I hope they don't send me back to zero grade. Or maybe I am very smart and I got to skip zero grade.

When I was little, like two years ago, I thought my real big name was "Jo Jo Makoons Azure Get to Your Room!" But that is very silly. Mama only calls me that when I'm in trouble.

My real big name is Josephine Makoons Azure. Moushoom, my grandpa, gave me the name Makoons since when I was a baby I would say, "Grrrr . . . ," like a growl. My baby hair was short and black—just like a little bear cub! Moushoom died, but I can still hear him when I'm out picking juneberries. It's a little tickle whisper that kisses my forehead from the wind.

My middle name is Makoons. You say *Makoons* like this: ma-KOONS.

I like to wear my hair with little bear ears. It is my bear hair. And it is very pretty.

Moushoom means "grandpa" in the Michif language. Michif is one kind of Native American language. It is a language made from words that are Cree, French, and Ojibwe. We speak very many languages on our reservation.

Ojibwe is my Native American tribe. You say it like this: oh-JIB-way. See? Ojibwe. Remember? I'm a member of the Pembina Ojibwe Nation. I live on the Pembina Ojibwe Reservation. I like to learn to speak Ojibwe and Michif.

Moushoom, *Grandpa*, told me it's good to

know our language. Then, when we speak it, our land will hear us and remember us.

I hope our land remembers that I do not like the zagimeg—*mosquitoes*.

When I tiptoe around my backyard I say, "Gaawiin zagimeg." *No mosquito.* I do it many times because sometimes people don't listen to me. I think the land will listen to me.

Kokum, *Grandma*, said the zagimeg like me because I am so sweet. My kokum is very smart. And pretty. And gives me cherry Life Savers when Mama isn't looking.

After I gave Bill's letters to Mama, I wanted to go play outside, but saw something sparkly on the kitchen table. It was a very shiny letter. But not from Bill. Bill's letters are white and not pretty.

"Mama, what is that letter?"

"My girl, which one?" she asked.

"That one." I lip-pointed to the one with the shiny paper envelope.

"Hmm?" Mama wrinkled her eyes.

I held up the envelope. It was see-through-ish and had glitter on it. You can tell if something is important because it has glitter all over it. Just like unicorn fur.

The envelope is very beautiful. You have to hold pretty things very softly.

Kokum took the letter and opened it. "Finally, it's Auntie Anne's wedding invitation!"

you are invited to the
wedding
of
ANNE & JEFFERY

I love Auntie Anne! She made my beary cute bedspread. Sewing is how she shows her love. Every night she gives me a blanket hug.

Mama looked at the letter. "It's from out of state. Not on our Pembina reservation."

I have been to a wedding here on our reservation. It was very fun. There was an announcement in the newspaper, and everyone brought food to share.

Then Mama gave a low whistle. "Boy, won't this be a fancy wedding! Wedding, a sit-down dinner, and a dance with a real live band! And it's so far away! It's almost a whole day's drive to get there," Mama said.

"Eya, *yes*," Kokum answered. "And we're going! It'll be an adventure."

"But it will cost so much," Mama said with her forehead crunched. She does this crunchy forehead a lot when she reads Bill's letters.

Kokum whispered, "My girl, that's why I have a rainy-day fund. We're going!"

I went to the window to see the rain. But it

was all sunny. Sometimes I wonder about how my grandma thinks. "No rain here, Kokum!"

"Oh, Jo Jo, 'saving for a rainy day' means to keep money for something in the future."

Like maybe buying more umbrellas?

I just heard the best word: *fancy.* I know how to do a lot of things. Like jump rope, play with dolls, and spit my peas in my milk glass at dinner so Mama thinks I ate them. That is why I always ask to clear the dishes when we have peas for supper.

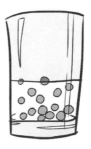

But, there's one thing I don't know how to do at all. If I'm going to a fancy wedding, I need to learn how to be fancy. I wonder—how do you be fancy?

Fancy Pants

I need to find out how to be fancy. How do you talk and eat fancy? How do you dress fancy? And what do you *do* at a fancy wedding?

I will need to use my favorite super-special sparkly purple unicorn notebook I got for my birthday from my Auntie Anne. I can learn how to be fancy. It is a notebook for me to write things that are secret. Shiny, sparkly things keep secrets very good. Mimi told me so.

Do you know how to keep a secret? It is very

important to only tell secrets to best friends. And a sparkly purple unicorn notebook.

Mimi is my best home friend. I tell her a lot of secrets. Like how to make splash sounds in the bathtub with my hands when I'm supposed to be washing up (so I can just sit and make up stories for Mimi, who sits on the bath rug next to me). Mama keeps saying she can't figure out why I'm still "ripe" when I take so many baths. It must be because I don't use soap sometimes when Mama isn't looking. But Mimi likes my stories. And Mimi doesn't say I am "ripe."

I love Mimi.

"Meow-or," she says when she wants to hear more stories. Mimi is a very good listener. She is very lucky because she can give herself a bath. I have tried to lick my own hands to clean them, too, but Mama says that is not a good idea.

I think it is a cat-tastic idea.

Every Monday morning Mama and Mimi have to remind me that it's time for school again. I like school, but I wish there was more time for lunch and recess. Those are the good parts.

The bus to school stops in front of my house. My grandma's job is to walk me to the bus stop. She is a very hard worker. I think she should get a raise.

"My girl," Kokum said that Monday morning at the bus stop, "remember to be helpful to

the little ones on the bus."

"Yes, Kokum, I always do! I even help get the spitballs out of their hair after Up-Chuck chucks them."

Up-Chuck is a person in my class. His real name is just Chuck. But I call him Up-Chuck because the first day of kindergarten last year he threw up. My teacher says I shouldn't call him that, but Up-Chuck always does a big belly laugh when I say it.

When Up-Chuck walked to the bus stop just then, Kokum made her squinty eyes at him. And lip-pointed. "My boy, no spit wads."

I am glad to be *helpful* when I tell on Up-Chuck. I think he agreed with this because he kept staring at me during the bus ride. Staring means you agree.

I meet my best school friend, Fern, every morning by the water fountain. We hold hands and walk to our classroom together. That is what best school friends do.

"Aaniin, children," said Teacher.

"Aaniin!" we both said to Teacher as we walked through the classroom door.

Teacher tries very hard to speak our Ojibwe language, but he is not very good. I told this to Mama, but she said I need to be kind to people and not tell them they are bad at things.

Teacher is not good at all at speaking Ojibwe. He tries, so it is okay. Teacher is not Ojibwe. He calls himself "white." But he really should work on his Ojibwe language skills.

They are very poor. I would not give him a sticker.

I wonder if that's why he stays after school when we leave.

I have to sit with Brie at school sometimes. Brie, who is not a best school friend, wears very pretty clothes. But she does not talk very pretty.

"Jo Jo, I can't see the board. Move your chair," Brie whispered.

I like to be *helpful.* "Move my chair, *what,* Brie?"

"Jo Jo, move your chair over *there.*" Brie lip-pointed to a spot next to her desk.

"No, Brie. Move my chair, *please.*"

Brie must have agreed I was being *helpful* because she stared at me for a long time.

I looked over at Brie's clothes. Her pants have yellow hearts and stars. That looks pretty. And fancy. She also moves her fingers fancy.

Putting pinkies up when you write must be fancy.

I don't know anything about being fancy. Today I started taking notes in my favorite purple unicorn notebook on questions and answers about how to be fancy.

HOW DO YOU BE FANCY?
THIS IS HOW YOU ARE FANCY

1. Find out how to be fancy (without Brie knowing).

   Put pinkies up when writing.

2. How do you eat fancy?

3. How do you look fancy?

4. What do you do at a fancy wedding?

Pie, Oh My!

That morning at math time, Teacher wanted us to practice counting in different ways. So we sat at our tables and worked on math. I still had to sit with Brie. Again. And Penny and Joe. We sit at the blue circle table. That really is the kids-who-can't-count-to-100-yet table.

Teacher clapped his hands just then.

"Class, we will be doing some fun math! We will be using food and math together."

Up-Chuck asked, "Do we get to eat food during math?"

"No, we will just be using food words in math today."

That did not sound like fun. Maybe Teacher does not know what *fun* is.

Fun is *eating* food, not just talking about it. Fun is playing with Mimi, Fern, or even Up-Chuck (but don't tell him I said so).

"Students, please take out your math notebooks and let's have some fun!"

I took out my math notebook. It is not very pretty. It is gray. I do not like gray, but it looks good on Kokum's hair. She has gray hair with silver highlights.

"Okay, children, how many letters does the word *apple* have?"

Fern whispered, "Five." Teacher nodded. Fern is very quiet sometimes, but her smile is very loud.

"Yes, good! Okay, class, here is a hard one. How many letters does *blueberry pie* have?"

Up-Chuck answered, "Eleven?"

"No, but close! Why don't you look it up,

Chuck?" Teacher looked at me quickly. He does not like it when I call Up-Chuck Up-Chuck. But that is his name. And Teacher just used it, too.

"No, I meant to say, Chuck, can you use the dictionary to look up the word for us?" Teacher said.

I did not know why Teacher made such a big mistake. I decided to be *helpful.*

"Teacher, *blueberry pie* has forty-seven letters." I tilted my head. When you tilt your head, it means you are being *helpful.*

"Jo Jo, no, it does not," Brie said. She said it very loud. And very un-nice.

Teacher said, "No, Jo Jo, that is very wrong. *Blueberry pie* certainly does not have forty-seven letters!"

"Yes, it does. My moushoom said so before he died last year. And Moushoom was always right."

Teacher's forehead started to get the bulgy vein. It looks like a purple river under his forehead. It is not a pretty purple.

"Well, no, Jo Jo. That's not true," Teacher said.

Some of the students looked at me with fast blinking. Blinky eyes mean they believe you.

I tilted my head, to be *helpful*, and shook my head back and forth again.

Teacher looked at me. He put his hands on his hips with his elbows pointed out.

Oh no. Teacher was making triangle arms. Triangle arms mean you are *very* mad.

"But my moushoom said it's good to know our Native language. Then, when we speak it, our land will hear us and remember us," I said.

"Well, I . . . ," Teacher said.

"So, in our language, *miini-baashkiminasigani-biitoosijigani-bakwezhigan* is how you say 'blueberry pie.'"

I gave Teacher a very big gum smile to show I helped him.

He gave me a very big stare. So he agrees with me! *Blueberry pie* has forty-seven letters.

Maybe using big, long words is how to be fancy?

HOW DO YOU BE FANCY?
THIS IS HOW YOU ARE FANCY

1. Find out how to be fancy (without Brie knowing).

   Put pinkies up when writing.

2. How do you eat fancy?

   Use very big food words to talk fancy.

3. How do you look fancy?

4. What do you do at a fancy wedding?

4

Dance Machine

Sometimes I like to eat butter. Just by itself. Just a little finger dip. It is best warm and squishy. Mimi thinks so, too. She always licks it right from my finger, because sometimes I sneak it to her under the table at home.

"Jo Jo, stop feeding Mimi," Mama always says.

Well, if they would feed Mimi better, I would not have to. All they give Mimi are pellets. Pellets that are a bit stinky. And, well, pellets.

But I think butter must be fancy because it is in a shiny gold wrapping. It is like food glitter.

Saturday, there is no school, but it's a Jo Jo workday. Sunday is my favorite day. And June, July, and August.

Saturday is chore day at my house. Chores are when you work for free because grown-ups say you have to.

"My girl, will you help me clean the basement?" Kokum asked me.

I do not enjoy chores, but I enjoy my kokum. "Eya, Mimi can help us, too!"

Kokum and Mama looked at each other. When grown-ups look at each other silently, it means they are proud of you.

I took the things off the shelf so Kokum could dust it. Why does she call it "dust"? She is taking the dust off, so it should be called "undusting."

Kokum likes to listen to the radio when she cleans. Her favorite is Native hip-hop. But sometimes she has to mute grown-up words in the songs when I'm around. She is very fast at hitting the mute button!

Hmmm. I watched her reach back and forth to undust the shelves.

"Okay, Jo Jo, let's vacuum the carpet. Can you please plug in the vacuum?"

"Eya!" I am so *helpful.*

I watched her move her arm front and back.

She vacuumed and made carpet roads. *Hmmm.*

"Okay, last chore, my girl. Let's fold laundry!"

My laundry job is to fold the socks. I have to find one sock and its best friend, and wrap them together in a hug.

I watched Kokum move her arms left and right, up and down, as she folded clothes. *Hmmm.*

"Kokum, did you say there will be dancing at Auntie Anne's fancy wedding?"

"Yes, oh, and it will be fun!"

I did not know that Kokum has the moves.

HOW DO YOU BE FANCY?
THIS IS HOW YOU ARE FANCY

1. Find out how to be fancy (without Brie knowing).

   Put pinkies up when writing.

2. How do you eat fancy?

   Use very big food words to talk fancy.

3. How do you look fancy?

4. What do you do at a fancy wedding?

   Dancing at a wedding is fancy.
   Do chores to music. Act out the
   chores over and over.
   Undust the shelves, move the
   vacuum, fold the laundry.

5

Alphabet Parade

Yesterday morning on the bus, my bus friend, Ferris, let me have the window seat. He was very nice to let me do that. So nice that I gave him the tuna-fish sandwich Mama packed for my lunch.

"Ferris, what do you know about fancy things, like glitter and stuff?" I asked.

"Well, glitter comes from plastic flakes, I think. Or maybe from tinfoil. But glitter is not good for the ocean. It sticks to the fish."

Ferris is so not right. But I'm trying to

learn about fancy things.

"I think glitter comes from unicorn sneezes," I said.

"More like unicorn farts."

I pinched my lips together and looked away. That is how to tell someone they are wrong, but I am still being nice.

It is a *helpful* way to let him know he is wrong. Again.

Fern and Lilly were waiting for me when I got off the bus. We walked to our classroom together holding hands.

"Boozhoo, children. Are you ready for our alphabet parade?" Teacher said as we walked in the door.

"Boozhoo. Yes, we are!" we said.

Today is the day our class gets to have an alphabet parade around the school. Last week Teacher gave each of us a letter. We worked all week to make a poster of our letter.

"Okay, children, let's line up so we can

begin our parade."

Susan was first in line because she got the letter *A*. Her poster was very beautiful. She drew an anteater, an acorn, and ants.

Makwa was after Susan. His poster had pictures of bears, burned toast, and butter.

He is a very fancy artist! Yay for butter!

I was near the end of the line. Teacher gave me the letter *U*. I worked very hard to make my alphabet parade poster. I am good at art.

"Jo Jo, do you know that *U* is the *ugliest* letter of the alphabet? Of all the vowels, it is the ickiest," Brie whispered behind me.

My mouth felt very sad. And my eyes started to sting.

But then I thought very hard and looked up to the ceiling. That is where you find many good ideas.

I looked at Brie, put my hands on my hips, elbows out, and made triangle arms like when Teacher was mad. I said, "Oh, do you mean words like unfriendly, upset, unhappy, undies, ugl—?"

"Teacher! Jo Jo is being mean to me!"

Teacher walked back to the end of the alphabet parade line. "Oh, Jo Jo, what are you saying?"

"Well, Brie does not like my letter *U*. I said I have the prettiest letter. Unicorns would not live without my letter!"

Teacher rolled his eyes. He must not believe me! Rolling your eyes means you don't believe someone.

Ferris snuck out of line. "Here, Jo Jo, put this on your poster. Right by the unicorn you drew."

I looked at what he gave me. It looked like

glitter! So pretty. And fancy. And made with ripped-up tin foil from the tuna sandwich I gave him.

It was a little tuna-stinky. But it was glitter-ish!

"Miigwech, Ferris! You are so very *helpful*," I said in a very loud whisper next to Brie's ear.

We walked around the school with our alphabet posters. Some children loved my *U* poster. I knew that because they stared at me. Remember, staring means you agree!

But everyone clapped for Fern's *O* poster. She drew all *O* words in Ojibwe. I gave her blinky eyes (which means you are very serious and full of truth) and said, "Oh, Fern, this is the alphabetest poster ever!"

Fern gave me her very loud smile. She is such a nice school best friend.

We went to lunch after the parade. I like to sit by Fern at lunch, but she had to eat with

the principal, Ms. Whirl Wind Horse. Teacher said, "Fern, our principal would like to talk to you about your wonderful *O* alphabet poster."

Why would anyone want to eat with grown-ups at school? Poor Fern.

I was last in the line to find a seat in the lunchroom. The only place left was next to Brie.

Poor me.

"Jo Jo, do you want some of my peanut butter sandwich?" Penny asked across the table.

Penny makes so much sense.

"Miigwech, Penny!" I said with a big gum smile.

I looked at her earrings. They were dangly, beaded, and shiny. And very pretty. They looked fancy.

But I do not have any big earrings. *Hmmm, how can I wear fancy earrings?*

HOW DO YOU BE FANCY?
THIS IS HOW YOU ARE FANCY

1. Find out how to be fancy (without Brie knowing).

> Put pinkies up when writing.
> Shiny things = fancy things.

2. How do you eat fancy?

> Use very big food words to talk fancy.

3. How do you look fancy?

> Pretty earrings make you look fancy.

4. What do you do at a fancy wedding?

> Dancing at a wedding is fancy.
> Do chores to music. Act out the
> chores over and over.
> Undust the shelves, move the
> vacuum, fold the laundry.

Math A-Go-Go

On Wednesday I gave Teacher a note about our trip to Auntie Anne's wedding.

"Excuse me, but I have a note from my mama," I said.

Teacher read it and looked like he wanted to cry. Must be tears of sadness. "Oh, you'll be missing school for two days? Oh, Jo Jo, well, that's . . . I . . ."

It will be very hard for him to teach without me for two whole days!

Teacher gave me homework to do when I'm gone. But I will not *be* at home. So I tried to be *helpful*. "But, shouldn't I be doing work for on the go? Like math a-go-go?"

Teacher gave me an eleven face. Do you know what an eleven face is? It is when eyebrows get all bunched-up and squished together when someone has a thinkie face. The skin folds like an eleven between their eyebrows. It means they are confused.

"Sure, Jo Jo, how about you practice math on your trip? Any way you want."

I gave Fern a big best-friend hug at the end of the school day.

"Have fun, Jo Jo," Fern said. Her smile was not so loud.

"I'll see you Monday, Fern." But my heart felt a little droopy. Why did my heart feel pushed-down and heavy-like?

* * *

At home that night I helped pack for our trip. It is good Mama and Kokum have me. I am so very *helpful.*

I packed my best doll (she has beading on her dress!), my coloring books, and a bag of pretty crayons that I sharpened (I kept the shavings in case I need lipstick for the fancy wedding).

Of course I packed Mimi's bear-ear headband that Auntie Anne sent for Mimi's birthday last year. Auntie Anne is beary nice. Mimi looked so cute with it on.

Auntie Anne is Mama's sister, and my auntie. So that means she is Mimi's auntie, too!

"Mama, where is Mimi's bag? I can help her pack."

Mama didn't answer, but she looked a long time at Kokum without saying anything. When grown-ups do this, it means they're proud of you.

They must be proud that I'm being so helpful *packing for Mimi.*

pretty crayons

"My girl," Kokum said. "Well, see, Mimi isn't coming on our trip. Cats don't travel well, dear. At least Mimi doesn't."

No! My eyes started to get sting-y. Big fatty tears jumped out of my eyes.

Why is Mama talking about forgetting to pack things? We can't forget Mimi!

"But I've never been without my best home friend. We *can't* leave Mimi!"

Mama hugged me. "Jo Jo, sometimes we have to leave things behind so we can have new adventures."

Kokum lip-pointed to Mimi. "My girl, do you know how you felt last winter when your tummy hurt and you were sick? Well, Mimi's tummy doesn't like being in the car. She wouldn't be happy."

Mama said, "Jo Jo, the neighbor will check on Mimi to make sure she has food and water while we're gone."

I looked at Mimi. She never lies to me. "Mimi, do you want to stay at home?"

We got up very early the next morning. My toy bag and my super-special shiny notebook were all packed.

I gave Mimi a very big best-home-friend hug. She had her back to me. I think she must have been crying kitty tears.

"Let's go!" Mama said when we pulled out of the driveway.

"Let's go!" Kokum said.

I just looked back at the window. *Mimi, I miss you already.*

After I dried my big, fat, wet tears, I started to get excited. We were finally going to my auntie's wedding very many hours away! It's always good to learn about visiting foreign places. Like Wisconsin.

Auntie Anne moved off our reservation a few years ago to the big city of Madison. She is a guidance counselor.

There will be different things to eat. I have to know how to order food that is special to that place. And I need to use big fancy Wisconsin manners.

Mama said Wisconsin is the "Dairy State,"

so they must eat a lot of cheese. I practiced how to order my breakfast on the drive. "Yes, miss, may I please have some cheese in my oatmeal?"

It is very nice to eat like the locals.

I needed to do my schoolwork. I took out my super-special shiny notebook so I could do math a-go-go.

"Seventy-five," I said.

Then I said, "Seventy-six."

Then I said, "Seventy-seven."

I kept up my math a-go-go like this for a while.

"Jo Jo, what are you doing?" Kokum asked.

"I am doing the work Teacher said to do. I'm counting each of those shiny green number signs on the side of the road."

"Jo Jo, those are mile markers. There are hundreds of them. We have over two hundred miles to go."

"Okay," I said. "Seventy-nine . . . eighty . . . eighty-one . . ."

"Let's not do that, my girl," Mama said.

"But, are you saying I *shouldn't* do my schoolwork? Teacher will *not* like that." His bulgy-outie vein in his forehead might come out.

Mama and Kokum looked at each other without saying anything. And did it again. And again.

They are so proud of me for doing my math a-go-go!

Eggs and an Auntie

We got to our hotel room. It was so big! I even got my own bed. It was so big I could do snow-angel swishes on it.

"Jo Jo, it's late, so it's time to get ready for bed," Mama said.

"But I'm hungry."

Kokum reached into her purse. She rubbed my tummy and whispered, "Oh, little Makoons is rumbly in there tonight, my girl. It's growling again." Kokum kissed me. "Maybe a snack will quiet little Makoons?"

Kokum gave me a snack from her purse. You must become a grandma when you start to carry snacks around for everyone.

I missed Mimi so much. We called our house before bed, after Mama saw my big fat tears, but Mimi did not pick up the phone.

"Jo Jo, that means Mimi is sleeping, which is good!" she said.

Well, okay. It is good to let Mimi sleep. She is what Kokum calls "a crabby cat."

I slept a lot! Except Kokum does little puffy-outie breaths when she sleeps. But it sounds like very much sleep kisses.

We get to go out to eat for breakfast! Mama never lets us do that. But Auntie Anne is paying. Now I can practice some fancy Wisconsin manners.

"Jo Jo, look at how big you are!" Auntie Anne said when we walked into the restaurant. "Everyone, I'd like you to meet Jeffery, my soon-to-be husband!"

I gave her a super very big hug. She is very pretty. And nice. And smells like cotton candy.

This Jeffery guy could use a kokum to redo his braid. It is very messy.

* * *

The waitress came to our table. Everyone said what they would like.

"Okay, hon, what do you want?" Waitress said when she looked at me.

"I would like some eggs, please," I answered. I am trying out my best fancy manners.

"Okay, how do you like your eggs?"

I looked at Waitress. "Well, I haven't eaten them yet, so I do not *know* how I like them."

"Hon, I mean, how do you want them cooked?"

"Well, I would like them cooked on the stove." *Waitress is not very good.*

Everyone looked at me, and at Waitress. Back and forth. Back and forth.

"Well, dear, I mean how do you want the eggs *served?*"

What is going on here? Maybe it is time for me to be helpful. "Well, I would like them served on a plate," I said, tilting my head. Tilting your head means you are being *helpful.*

Mama said quickly, "She'll have eggs over-easy."

That must be the fancy way of saying yolky eggs. Mama knows what I like.

I gave Mama and Waitress a big gum smile so they would know I wasn't being mean.

Oh! Wait, I need to use big, long words so I can be fancy. Here in Wisconsin.

"And can I please also have some miini-baashkiminasigani - biitoosijigani-bakwezhigan?"

Waitress's eyebrows got bunched-up and

squished together. She made an eleven fore-head. Waitress was confused.

That Jeffery guy said, "Oh, but do you want ice cream with that, Jo Jo?" And he did a head-back laugh.

I like that Jeffery guy now. He speaks Ojibwe. It will be good for our land to hear him and remember us. And to know that we like pie. And big, long, fancy words.

Auntie Anne said something about how she had to be sure to leave a big tip. Not sure what that means, but wasn't I so *helpful* to Waitress?

And, we got pie! Oh my!

Wedding Ever After

It is Auntie Anne and that Jeffery's wedding day! That Jeffery guy is from the Turtle Mountain Band of Ojibwe in North Dakota. Mama said they are like close neighbors to our Pembina reservation. A close neighbor is one who gives out *good* Halloween candy. Not toothbrushes.

I was so excited that I got up early. But Mama said very loudly through the covers, "Jo Jo, it's three a.m.; it's not time to get up."

Well, it *is* Saturday, and it *is* wedding day.

So I stayed up and counted how many sleep kisses Kokum made until they both got up.

I do not know how to count to one hundred yet, but I counted her puffy-outie breaths to ninety-nine so many times! I also stood over Mama and counted her pretty gray hairs.

It is good to do my math a-go-go.

They *finally* got up, and now we have to get "ready." "Getting ready" means to try not to look like your everyday usual self.

Mama did very pretty braids in her hair and put on fancy beaded barrettes and ear-rings. Her dress was shiny blue with stripes. How pretty and fancy!

"Going to put my shapewear on in the bathroom," Kokum said.

Hmm, shapes? This is good to learn about for my math a-go-go.

"Kokum, what shape are you going to put on?" She would look very pretty in an oval or square.

She held up a long noodle thing. "This, my girl, is how I can still fit into my special dress." Kokum's eyes sparkled. "The dress was your moushoom's favorite."

I looked at the "shapewear" she held up. I have never seen a shape like *that* before.

But she came out with her dress on and was super really pretty! Her dress had shiny glitter buttons on it. It was very fancy! And she had lipstick on!

"Okay, little one, time for you to change," Mama said.

I changed into the dress she packed. But it was not fancy. And not very pretty.

My eyes started to sting again. *Everyone is fancy, but I am* not.

"My girl, what's the matter?" Mama and Kokum said as they hugged me.

I huffed an in-and-out breath. "I . . . I'm . . .

I'm not fancy. I'm not *fancy* for Auntie Anne's wedding! But everyone else will be! Even that Jeffery guy!"

I wished Mimi were with us. Or Fern. Or even Brie, who would tell me how to be fancy. Well, maybe not Brie.

I think about when Auntie Anne comes back every summer to dance in our Pembina reservation powwow. She is a jingle-dress dancer. That means her dress jingles help us to feel better.

Except, I do not feel better now. I want to be fancy so I can do something for *her*. On her and that Jeffery guy's marrying day.

"Jo Jo, we have to get to the ceremony. You look very nice," Mama whispered.

Nice is what cheese and butter tastes like. Nice is *not* fancy. "But I learned all about how to be fancy! It's not working."

Kokum gave me a pair of her sparkly clip-on

earrings. And they were glittery. And beautiful.

Mama made my bear hair extra puffy. And it was very Makoons. And attractive.

"Okay, let's go," I whispered. But I still did not *feel* fancy.

At the wedding we sat down in a "pew." But it was not stinky. I do not know why they always call it that. So far a pew has never been P.U.

But I have never sat in one with Up-Chuck.

Slow music started and people began walking down the middle church carpet road. I could see that Jeffery guy up front! His braid looked very nice. I wondered if his kokum did it for him.

Then we all stood, and everyone looked at the back of the church. I saw Auntie Anne! Oh, her dress was so very beautiful and fancy! It had shiny beads and very many glitter buttons.

I'm getting sleepy. Then I woke up leaning on Mama's arm.

They were doing the blanket ceremony. I heard Auntie Anne say, "I do." Wonder what the question was?

Pretty soon everyone followed her and that Jeffery guy out of the church. We went to something called a reception dinner. Kokum called it buy-dinner-for-your-annoying-family meal.

But she looked at me with a wink blink. That means it is a joke. Even though I don't get it.

I looked at everyone in their fanciness, and felt a little heart-pushed-down.

Wedding Crasher

I had the job of taking care of the guest book. That meant I had to make sure *everyone* signed their name. Or else they could not go to the wedding reception thing.

What an important wedding job I had!

I stood behind a little table with the fancy white guest book. Everyone lined up and I gave them a pen and lip-pointed to where they should sign.

"Sign here, please."

"Please sign in, cousin."

Kokum said all us Native people are related, so that means we all are cousins!

Most of the people already knew what to do, but some did not. Some did not even know to put up their pinky when writing. I helped them with that.

"Excuse me, kid, you *must* sign in," I said to be *helpful*.

"Um, yeah, well, my son is two years old. He doesn't have to sign in. Little Jimmy doesn't know how to write anyway," Lady said.

"I'll help him!" I grabbed a crayon from my pocket and gave it to Little Jimmy. He signed his name, but it just looked like a squiggle to me. He might need to go to zero grade soon.

Auntie Anne and that Jeffery guy came in together. She gave me a big hug. Auntie smelled so pretty and fancy.

"Jo Jo, you look so pretty!"

"Well, but I wanted to be fancy. Like *you*," I said quietly so that Jeffery guy couldn't hear.

"Oh, little Makoons, fancy isn't what you

look like on the outside. It's what you look like on the *inside*, my girl."

So my guts and bones need to be fancy?

Auntie Anne bopped my nose. "Jo Jo, you don't need to be fancy. It's more important to be you, Jo Jo. And to make your own rules about how to be fancy."

They both tried to walk past my table.

"Excuse me, but you need to sign the fancy guest book. It's my job, remember?" I tilted my head. That means you are being *helpful,* remember?

That Jeffery guy laughed and said, "Well, okay, sure, Jo Jo! Boy, you are just like a bouncer."

I do not know what bouncing has to do with this, but I do jump very high.

After everyone signed the guest book, I gave it to Mama to keep it safe. Sometimes I lose things, and this was a very important book. She patted my bear hair. "Miigwech, Jo Jo."

Auntie Anne said, "The music is starting soon, so everyone please eat up!"

I ran from Mama, Kokum, and the other elders to get them coffee or more cake. The cake was they what they called carrot cake. I would like to talk to the baker who thought vegetables go in cake. They do not.

"Miigwech, my girl," they all said. I started to feel my smile come back. Just a little.

Then the lights got kind of dark, and the music started. Auntie Anne and that husband Jeffery guy danced first. They had very much love in their eyes. And feet.

Everybody got to dance then.

"Kokum, let's go dance!" I said.

"Oh, my girl, I don't dance for a year. It's how I show my feelings for losing Moushoom." I looked at my kokum and gave her a very big Jo Jo hug. And blinked my eyes on her arm. That is a fluffy butterfly hug and means you love someone very much.

"But who will dance with me? Mama?"

Mama laughed and turned to talk to the other elders. "You can go, Jo Jo. Have fun."

I had all these fancy dance moves I learned from chores. I could not sit still.

Then I saw lots of my little cousins jumping up and down by their parents. *They need some dance move lessons.*

One of the little cousins bumped into a table. *Crash!* A fancy glass fell and broke into tiny, shiny pieces.

"Pretty!" little cousin Kimber said, reaching for the glass.

She's going to cut her fingers trying to pick it up. Oh no!

"Come on, my girl, time to go drink some water," I said as I held her hand and told a grown-up about the broken glass so they could clean it up.

I showed the little ones, and some big ones, how to have the dance moves, too! The

wedding was so fun! So fun my eyes began to feel heavy.

"Oh, Jo Jo, you just look so fancy! Did you have fun?" Auntie Anne said as we were leaving.

"Eya, Auntie. I thought I did want to be fancy, except I liked something else even *better*. I liked to be *helpful*. It made my inside, you know, *guts and bones*, feel happier."

When I went back to school Monday, I gave my whole class very big hugs. They must have missed me so much! I even gave one to Brie, but only a side hug so I wouldn't give her all my happiness. Happiness leaks out when you give hugs. Teacher was very glad to have me back, too, because he kept staring out the window shaking his head when I walked into the classroom!

I took out my alphabet parade *U* poster

and showed everyone my math a-go-go on the back. I think Teacher was so very happy. I was so *helpful* to show Teacher about my math a-go-go.

JO JO'S GLOSSARY

A glossary is a very fancy word for a small dictionary. It is where you can learn about new words and how to say them. These are some Ojibwe and Michif words from this story:

aaniin (AH-neen): hello, greetings

boozhoo (BOO-zhoo): hello, greetings

eya (ee-YEH): yes

gaawiin (gah-WEEN): no

kokum (KUH-kum): Michif word for grandma

miigwech (mee-GWECH): thank you

miini-baashkiminasigani-biitoosijigani-bakwezhigan (mii-ni-baash-ki-mi-na-si-ga-ni-bii-too-si-ji-ga-ni-ba-kwe-zhi-gan): blueberry pie

moushoom (MUH-shoom): Michif word for grandpa

makoons (ma-KOONS): little bear cub

Ojibwe (oh-JIB-way): the name of my Native American Nation

zagimeg (zah-i-MAY): many mosquitoes

AUTHOR'S NOTE

The Ojibwe people belong to many Bands (or groups) and Nations. I am part of the Pembina Band of Ojibwe. My reservation is the Turtle Mountain reservation in North Dakota. It is the current land for the Turtle Mountain Band of Ojibwe.

The Ojibwe Nations are within the borders of the United States and Canada. Some of our Ojibwe reservations are within the borders of North Dakota, Wisconsin, Minnesota, and Michigan. Just like Jo Jo said, we speak Ojibwe, but also many other dialects, or versions, of it. My Turtle Mountain reservation uses Ojibwe and Michif.

Dear Reader,

My, that Jo Jo Makoons sure is fancy! But as Auntie Anne says, it's even more important that Jo Jo is Jo Jo—that she's her glorious self. Just like it's important that you are you!

As for fancy, Jo Jo can be fancy when she's joking with Up-Chuck or missing Mimi or spending time with Fern and Brie or rooting for Teacher to do better. She can be fancy at a wedding, telling her cousins where to sign the guest book. She can be fancy whenever she wants! Just like you, Jo Jo can make her own rules for fanciness!

My rule is: Anyone who reads this whole book is as fancy as can be.

If I had extra banana stickers, I'd give them to you to use as fancy earrings!

Have you read any other stories about Jo Jo or other Ojibwe heroes? How about characters from other Indigenous Nations? I hope this book encourages you to read more.

Jo Jo Makoons: Fancy Pants is written by Dawn Quigley, illustrated by Tara Audibert, and published by Heartdrum, a Native-focused imprint of HarperCollins Children's Books. An imprint is like a little umbrella under the bigger umbrella of a publishing company. We publish stories by Native writers and artists about Native heroes who are kids like you.

Keep reading and have fun being fancy, whatever that means to you!

Be sure to look for more books in the Jo Jo Makoons series, too!

Thank you for reading,
Cynthia Leitich Smith

DAWN QUIGLEY is a citizen of the Turtle Mountain Band of Ojibwe, North Dakota. She is the author of another book about Jo Jo Makoons, *Jo Jo Makoons: The Used-to-Be Best Friend*. Her debut YA novel, *Apple in the Middle*, was awarded an AILA American Indian Youth Literature Honor. She is a PhD education university faculty member and a former K–12 reading and English teacher, as well as Indian Education program codirector. Dawn lives in Minnesota with her family. You can find her online at www.dawnquigley.com.

TARA AUDIBERT is a multidisciplinary artist, filmmaker, cartoonist, animator, and podcaster. She owns and runs Moxy Fox Studio, where she creates her award-winning works, including the animated short film *The Importance of Dreaming*, the comics *This Place: 150 Years Retold* and *Lost Innocence*, and "Nitap: Legends of the First Nations," an animated storytelling app. She is of Wolastoqey/French heritage and resides in Sunny Corner, New Brunswick, Canada. You can find her online at www.moxyfox.ca.

CYNTHIA LEITICH SMITH is a best-selling, acclaimed author of books for all ages, including *Rain Is Not My Indian Name, Indian Shoes, Jingle Dancer, Hearts Unbroken*, and *Sisters of the Neversea*. She is also the editor of the anthology *Ancestor Approved*. Cynthia is the author-curator of Heartdrum, a Native-focused imprint at HarperCollins Children's Books, and is the Katherine Paterson Endowed Chair at Vermont College of Fine Arts. She is a citizen of the Muscogee Nation and lives in Austin, Texas. You can visit her online at www.cynthialeitichsmith.com.

In 2014, **WE NEED DIVERSE BOOKS** (WNDB) began as a simple hashtag on Twitter. The social media campaign soon grew into a 501(c)(3) nonprofit with a team that spans the globe. WNDB is supported by a network of writers, illustrators, agents, editors, teachers, librarians, and book lovers, all united under the same goal—to create a world where every child can see themselves in the pages of a book. You can learn more about WNDB programs at www.diversebooks.org.

Read on for a peek at
Jo Jo's first adventure!

DAWN QUIGLEY

JoJo Makoons

THE USED-TO-BE BEST FRIEND

ILLUSTRATED BY TARA AUDIBERT

Best Friend #1

"Goodbye, Mimi," I said as I walked past her on the way toward the front door.

Mimi:

"I said *goodbye*, Mimi! I'll miss you!" I even threw some air kisses to her.

Mimi only turned her head away from me.

"Mimi, you will always be my best friend number one!"

Mimi:

Why is it she won't ever reply? Or let me

know she'll miss *me* when I'm gone? I know I'll miss her.

We do this every day. 'Cause I have to leave every day. Well, most days. Mama says it's the law.

There should be a law about not saying goodbye to your first *best friend*. The one who has to go to school *every* day. Every day!

I think I would like more friends. At least ones who will answer me.

But cats are *very* good home friends. They

are already potty-trained. They are very clean. And they even will take you on a walk.

I have a home best friend, and I used to have a school best friend.

But I don't think my school best friend wants to be *my* best friend anymore. I think I need more pals. Just in case.

Let me tell you about myself. I am seven years old and in the first grade. My name is Jo Jo Makoons Azure. You wanna know another way of saying that, in Ojibwe? (That's the name of my Native American tribe!) Try saying: "Jo Jo Makoons Azure nindizhinikaaz."

Big last word, right? You sound out that last word like this: nin-DEZH-in-i-kauz.

Got it? If you can say *Tyrannosaurus rex*, you can say *nindizhinikaaz*.

But my real big name is Josephine Makoons Azure. Mama says Moushoom gave me the name Makoons because when I was a baby,

I growled and had short black hair—just like a little bear cub! You say *Makoons* like this: ma-KOONS.

Do you wanna know what *moushoom* means? It means "grandpa" in the Michif language. Michif is one kind of Native American language. But it is a language made from words that are Cree, French, and Ojibwe. We speak many languages on our reservation.

Ojibwe is my Native American tribe. You say it like this: oh-JIB-way. See? Ojibwe.

I'm learning my Ojibwe language because I'm a member of the Pembina Ojibwe Nation. I like to learn to speak Ojibwe and Michif.

I asked Mama, "What's the difference between Ojibwe and Michif?"

"Well, my girl, think of Michif like a part of the big, beautiful Ojibwe world."

* * *